Baseball:
Becoming a Great Hitter

By Ron Fitzgerald

HIGH
interest
books

Children's Press
A Division of Grolier Publishing
New York / London / Hong Kong / Sydney
Danbury, Connecticut

A special thanks to Saint Patrick High School in Elizabeth, New Jersey

Book Design: Nelson Sa
Contributing Editor: Rob Kirkpatrick

Photo Credits: Cover © Angelo Barros and Nelson Sa; p. 5 © Ezro Shaw/All Sport; p. 7 © Andy Lyons/All Sport; p. 8 © Angelo Barros and Nelson Sa; p. 11 © M. David Leeds/All Sport; pp. 12, 14, 15, 16, 17, 18, 19 © Angelo Barros and Nelson Sa; p. 21 © Scott Halleran/All Sport; p. 22 © Tom Hauck/All Sport; p. 25 © Robert Laberge/All Sport; p. 27 © Angelo Barros and Nelson Sa; pp. 28, 30 © Jed Jacobsohn/All Sport; pp. 33, 34, 35 © Angelo Barros and Nelson Sa; p. 36 © Matthew Stockman/All Sport; p. 39 © Angelo Barros and Nelson Sa; p. 41 © Todd Warshaw/All Sport.

Visit Children's Press on the Internet at:
http://publishing.grolier.com

Library of Congress Cataloging-in-Publication Data

Fitzgerald, Ron.
　Baseball: Becoming a great hitter / by Ron Fitzgerald.
　　p. cm. – (Sports clinic)
　Includes bibliographical references and index.
　Summary: Explains how to hit a baseball, including how to hold and swing a bat.
　ISBN 0-516-23361-0 (lib. bdg.) – ISBN 0-516-23561-3 (pbk.)
　1. Batting (Baseball)—Juvenile literature. [1. Batting (Baseball) 2. Baseball.] I. Title: Becoming a great hitter. II. Title. III. Series.

GV869.F57 2000
796.357'26—dc21

00-026220

CONTENTS

INTRODUCTION

"The hardest thing to do is to hit a round baseball with a round bat, squarely."
— Ted Williams, American League MVP (1946, 1949)

Many people think that hitting a baseball is the hardest thing to do in all of sports. A batter has less than a second to decide to swing, swing the bat, and make solid contact with the ball. If you don't have good batting skills, you will be lucky if you even touch the ball. But if you develop a good stance, a good swing, and good concentration, you can be a good hitter.

If hitting does not come naturally to you, don't worry. Becoming a great hitter takes years of practice. You will have to hit a lot of balls both in practices and games. You may have to take a lot of swings in batting cages. Even when you start hitting the ball well,

Hitting a baseball is one of the toughest jobs in sports.

4

you need to keep practicing. You want to hold onto your hitting skills and keep improving them. Even Major League hitters never stop practicing and learning.

Hitting a baseball is a challenging skill to learn. But it also can be fun. As you become a good hitter, you will enjoy being able to hit the best that a pitcher throws your way. A good hitter scares the other team. He uses the bat as a weapon in the game of baseball. This book is the user's guide to that weapon.

Even great hitters like the New York Mets's Mike Piazza spend years learning how to become great hitters.

BATTER UP!

Stepping up to the plate and hitting a ball is one of the best feelings in sports. It's not an easy thing to do, though. It can be a little scary the first time you step up to the plate. After all, the pitcher is throwing a small object as fast as he can. Don't worry. The pitcher is not trying to hit you. He is trying to throw the ball over home plate. Your job is to hit the ball.

CHOOSING A BAT

A batter with the wrong type of bat will not be a good hitter. There are many things that a player needs to think about when choosing a bat. There are long and short bats. There are heavy bats and light bats. Bats also can be made of different materials. By finding the right bat for you, you will have a better chance of hitting the ball.

The first step to becoming a good hitter is choosing the right bat.

Bat Secrets

Most wooden bats are made of wood from ash trees. Metal bats are made of different kinds of metals, such as aluminum and graphite.

Wood or Metal?

Bats are made of either wood or metal. Most high school and college players prefer to use metal bats. You can hit a baseball a little farther using a metal bat. Major League Baseball does not allow hitters to use metal bats. Minor-league players also have to use wooden bats.

There's a spot in the middle of a bat where the bat will hit the ball with the most force. This is called the sweet spot. Metal bats have a much bigger sweet spot than wooden bats do. Metal bats are much more solid than wooden bats. You can make good contact with almost any part of the barrel (thick part) of a metal bat.

A slugger such as Mark McGwire can hit the ball a long way if he makes contact with the sweet spot of the bat.

Batter Up!

Weighing In

Bats have different weights. Find a bat that is the right weight for you. Do not try to find the heaviest bat just so that you can impress your teammates. A good hitter is measured by his or her hits, not by the weight of his or her bat. If you are using a bat that is too heavy, you will not be able to swing correctly. You will have trouble bringing a heavy bat around in time to hit a pitch. If you do hit the ball, you are more likely to hit it weakly.

BASEBALL: BECOMING A GREAT HITTER

A bat that is too light is no better. Players who use bats that are too light will get the barrel of the bat out too soon during their swing. Their best hits usually will be fouls (balls hit outside the field of play). Right-handed batters will hit balls too far to the left. Left-handed batters will hit balls too far to the right.

Batter Up!

Try swinging different bats to find one that is the right weight for you. Look for a bat that you can swing comfortably. If you feel a bat dipping as you swing, it is too heavy for you. You want to have a good solid bat that you can swing directly at the ball.

The Size of Your Bat

Bats come in different lengths. Shorter bats are easier to swing. But longer bats help you to reach pitches on the outside of the strike zone.

Bat handles have different sizes, too. Some bats may have thick handles. Other bats may have thin handles. The size of a bat's handle affects how well you can grip the bat. If you have small hands, you may not be able to use a bat with a thick handle. If you have big hands, you could use a bat with a thicker handle.

GET A GRIP

The proper grip is important. A good grip means a quicker swing and more bat speed. More bat speed

Bats have different sizes and weights.
Find a bat that is right for you.

Figure 1: A proper grip is important.

means more hitting power. The standard baseball grip is fairly simple. If you are right-handed, place your right hand above your left hand on the bat. If you are left-handed, your left hand should be on top. Your bottom hand should rest on the knob, or base, of the bat (see figure 1). Do not squeeze the bat. Hold it loosely and curl your fingers.

Some batters line up all of their knuckles when they grip the bat . Others line up the knuckles of their bottom hand with the finger joints of their top hand. Still others grip the bat somewhere in between these two styles. Figure out which way is the most comfortable one for you.

Figure 2: Some hitters may need to choke up.

Choking Up

Sometimes, you may bat against a pitcher who can throw very fast. Or you may just have trouble making contact with the ball. If one of these things is happening to you, try placing your grip farther up the bat. This is called choking up.

To choke up, place your hands a couple of inches above the knob (see figure 2). Choking up gives you more control over the bat. You might not get as much power out of your swing, but you will be more likely to hit the pitch.

Choking up is not just for weak hitters. Many times, even home-run hitters in the major leagues choke up if they have two strikes. They do not want to get a third strike and strike out. They choke up to give themselves a better chance to hit the pitch.

THE STANCE

The place where you stand at the plate is called the batter's box. The batter's box is a rectangle on the side of the plate. There is a box on each side of the plate. One is for left-handed hitters, and one is for right-handed hitters. Usually, you want to stand so that your stronger (throwing) arm is closer to the catcher. Some hitters feel more comfortable in the other box, with their stronger arm closer to the pitcher. Some players learn how to hit in either box. They are called switch hitters.

Hitters stand in different places in the batter's box. Usually, the hitter stands directly beside the plate (see figure 3). This may change based on the pitcher. If the pitcher throws very fast pitches, you might want to stand deeper in the batter's box (closer to the catcher).

Figure 3: Usually, you should stand directly beside home plate.

16

Batter Up!

When you stand deeper in the box, you have a little more time to react to the pitch. If the pitcher throws a lot of curve balls or sinkers (pitches that sink as they approach the plate), try standing farther up in the box (closer to the pitcher). Standing closer helps you hit the pitch before it curves or drops away from you.

Wherever you stand, make sure that you can protect the whole plate. This means that you need to be able to hit both inside pitches (close to you) and outside pitches (away from you). When you first step up to the plate, try this test. Stand in the batter's box and try to touch the front, outside corner of the plate with the tip of your bat (see figure 4). You want to be able to touch the corner without bending your upper body over all the way. If you can, your bat will be able to hit any ball thrown in the strike zone. The next time you see a

Figure 4: You should be able to touch the outside of the plate.

BASEBALL: BECOMING A GREAT HITTER

Major League Baseball game, you may see hitters do this test before they get ready to hit.

Now you are ready to take your stance. Make sure that your head is turned toward the pitcher. Your chin should be close to your front shoulder (see figure 5). Do not tilt your head. Keep both eyes on the ball during the pitcher's windup and delivery with both eyes. Watching the ball is very important.

You are standing in the batter's box. The pitcher is on the mound. It's just about time for the showdown. Let's make sure you are in position to hit the ball with power when the ball arrives.

Figure 6: Bend your knees slightly during your stance.

Feet

Stand with your feet apart a little more than shoulder width. Point your toes toward the plate. Bend your knees slightly (see figure 6). Also, balance is important. Keep your weight on the inside balls of your feet for good balance.

Hands

As you hold the bat, your hands should be at about shoulder height. Hold your hands toward your back shoulder and a few inches away from your body. The bat should be sitting at a forty-five degree-angle from your body (see figure 5).

Figure 5: Hold your chin near your front shoulder, and hold the bat at approximately a forty-five-degree angle.

Different Stances

If you watch a baseball game, you will see that all players have different stances. Ted Williams once wrote, "Show me ten great hitters and I'll show you ten different styles." Some players hold the bat higher toward their heads. Some hold it farther back from their bodies. Some players spread their legs wide apart in the batter's box. Others wiggle the bat as they wait for the pitch. But if you were to look at a slow-motion video of just about any big-league player, you would find that they all come to a similar position just before swinging. Every successful hitter gets his bat, hands, and arms set just before swinging. The important thing is to find a stance that is comfortable for you.

Not all stances look alike.
Some batters have unusual-looking stances.

HERE COMES THE PITCH

You are in your stance. The pitcher goes into his windup. Your bat is up, and your elbows are down. Here comes the pitch. What do you do now?

THE STRIDE

Keep your weight back until the ball is on its way to the plate. Now stride (step) toward the ball with your front foot. As you stride forward, bring back the bat. This is called "cocking" your hands.

Striding brings your weight forward as you prepare to hit the pitch. Bringing your weight forward helps you to drive the bat through the strike zone with great speed. More bat speed means more hitting power.

The hitter strides (steps) forward to meet the pitch.

Do not rush your stride and step forward too soon. If you rush, you will have no power in your swing. You will end up swinging with your arms and not with your whole body. You have to time your stride with the arrival of the ball.

THE STRIKE ZONE

The ball is coming at you. You are striding toward the pitcher. It's time to take a swing, right?

Hold on. Make sure you are swinging at a good pitch. Do not swing at a pitch that is out of the strike zone. You are better off taking (not swinging at) the pitch. The umpire will call a bad pitch a "ball." If the pitcher throws you four balls, you get a walk (free trip to first base). If the pitcher is going to give you something for free, you might as well take it. Besides, it is usually easier to hit a strike (pitch that is in the strike zone).

Where Is the Strike Zone?

According to the official rules of Major League Baseball, the strike zone is the area over home plate

A good batter will swing only at pitches that are in the strike zone.

24

Here Comes The Pitch

DID YOU KNOW?

In order to swing on time, major leaguers have about 0.15 seconds per pitch to make up their minds whether to swing.

STRIKE ZONE

that starts below the batter's kneecaps. It reaches to at least the top of the batter's uniform pants. It can go as high as the top of the batter's shoulders (see figure 7). The home plate umpire decides the strike zone.

Each umpire's strike zone can be different. If the umpire has a large strike zone, it helps the pitcher. If the umpire has a small strike zone, it helps the batter. It may take some time during a game to locate a particular umpire's strike zone. If the umpire has a wide strike zone, the batter may want to swing at pitches that are just outside. On the other hand, if the umpire likes to call strikes on low pitches, the batter may want to swing at pitches that are below his or her knees.

For most hitters, the best pitch to hit is one that is in the center of the strike zone. This pitch is neither low nor high. It is neither inside nor outside. A pitch that is right down the center is the easiest to hit solidly. Players call this a "fat" pitch. Hitters get most of their hits when the ball is directly over the center of

Figure 7: The strike zone rises at least as high as the batter's waist, and may go as high as the batter's shoulders.

the plate. When you are up to bat, you may want to take a pitch or two and hope that the next pitch is a nice, fat, juicy one.

Remember, you only have a split second to decide whether to swing at a pitch. If you wait to decide before you make your stride, it will be too late. The ball will blow past you. You should stride forward on every pitch. Then, as the ball is on its way, decide whether to swing. If it is a fat pitch, you will be ready.

Great hitters such as Nomar Garciaparra can hit "fat" pitches a long way.

29

THREE

SWING AWAY!

OK, here comes a strike right down the middle. You are striding toward the pitcher. Now it's time to swing.

The swing begins as the stride ends. As your front foot lands, move your hands forward. Keep your head down and your chin tucked to your front shoulder. Be sure to keep your eyes on the ball. Bring the bat around in a powerful swing.

Many coaches will say you need a level swing. This is mostly true. You should not swing your bat way up high. If you swing up, it is harder to make contact with the ball. But because the pitcher is standing on a mound, the pitch travels to the plate at a slight downward angle. You will need to swing up, but only at a very slight angle.

Slugger Barry Bonds packs a lot of power into his swing.

As you swing, move your body with your arms. Turn your hips toward the ball. Your back foot turns, too. When you hit the ball, your arms should be making a "V" shape.

THE FOLLOW-THROUGH

Hold on, slugger! Don't start your home run trot until you finish your swing.

Make sure that you hit "through" the ball. Your swing does not end as soon as you hit the ball. Because you are putting so much energy into your swing, the follow-through happens naturally: Your arms keep swinging even after you hit the ball. Your hips open up to the pitcher. Your knees and belly button end up facing the pitcher (see figure 8).

Watch the pitch all the way into your bat. Your head should stay down as you finish your swing. If you get into the habit of looking up to see how far you've hit the ball, you will begin stepping away from the plate with your front foot as you swing. This is

Figure 8: As you follow through, your body ends up facing the pitcher.

called pulling off the ball. When you pull off the ball, you are less likely to hit it with the barrel of the bat.

Have you ever watched a golfer hit a golf ball? Good golfers keep their heads down for a moment even after they hit the ball. Major League hitters keep their heads down, too.

Two-Hand Finish

Players finish their swings differently. Most players keep both hands on the bat handle until the very end of the swing. After the batter hits the ball, his wrists turn over. His hands swing up and over his front shoulder. Usually, a batter gets the most power from his swing if he follows through with both hands (see figure 9).

Figure 9: The two-hand finish

The One-Hand Finish

As the batter hits the ball, the top hand comes off the bat. The bottom hand stays on the bat handle. The bottom hand follows through, and the top hand ends up close to or touching the batter's shoulder (see figure 10).

Some pro ball players like to use the one-hand finish. They feel it helps them to focus on the ball and to make contact. However, many younger players may find that they do not get enough power with a one-hand finish. You should practice to see which style works for you.

Swing Away!

DID YOU KNOW?

A player named Pete Gray played for the St. Louis Browns in 1945 even though he had only one arm.

TROUBLESHOOTING

Many people feel that hitting a baseball is the hardest thing to do in all of sports. It takes a lot of practice to be a great hitter. Good hitters work on their swings every day.

THE HIT LIST

Some players have a hard time learning how to swing properly. Even if you have a good swing, you may have times when you do not hit well. These times are called batting slumps. If you fall into a slump, go back to the basics. Make sure that you are using correct form in all parts of your swing.

The Baltimore Orioles's Cal Ripken's practice habits helped him get more than three thousand hits.

37

BASEBALL: BECOMING A GREAT HITTER

This checklist should get you going in the right direction:

• Move your hands.

As you start your swing, your hands move the knob of the bat out in front of you. Then, as you turn your hips, your hands pull the barrel around to smack the ball.

• Turn your hips.

Twist your hips as you bring the bat around. Your back knee will turn forward as your front leg straightens.

• Make contact.

Think about making a "V" with your arms. Your bottom arm should straighten as you pull the bat to meet the ball. Remember to keep your eyes on the ball. You cannot hit the ball if you aren't looking at it.

Look directly at the ball when you swing.

Swing Away!

• Keep your head down.

When you hit the ball, your head should be down. You should be looking at the ball as you hit it.

• Follow through.

Finish off your swing. Don't cut it short. Bring your hand (or hands) up past your head as you follow through.

• Head to the cages!

If you fall into a batting slump, go to a batting cage and practice your swing.

Great young hitters such as Alex Rodriguez bring excitement to the game.

barrel the thick part of the bat

batter's box the place where you stand when you
are up at bat

choke up to hold the bat a couple of inches above
the knob

grip the way you hold the bat

grounder a batted ball that rolls or bounces on the
ground

handle the place where you hold the bat with your
hands

knob the base of the bat

Major League Baseball the highest level of
professional baseball in North America

minor leagues leagues in which players hope to develop the skills needed in the Major Leagues

one-hand finish when you finish your swing with only one hand on the bat handle

sweet spot the place on a bat where a ball is hit with the most force

stance the manner in which you stand in the batter's box

stride the little step you take before you swing the bat

strike zone the area over home plate where a pitch is called a strike

two-hand finish when you complete a swing with both hands on the bat handle

FOR FURTHER READING

Jordan, Godfrey P. *Kid's Book of Baseball Revised and Updated: Hitting, Fielding, and the Rules of the Game.* Secaucus, NJ: Carol Publishing Group, 1999.

McCarthy, John P., Jr. *Youth Baseball: The Guide for Coaches and Parents.* 2nd ed. Cincinnati: Betterway Books, 1989.

Stewart, John. *The Baseball Clinic: Skills and Drills for Better Baseball—a Handbook for Players and Coaches.* Short Hills, NJ: Buford Books, 1999.

Williams, Ted, and John Underwood. *The Science of Hitting.* New York: Fireside, 1986.

ORGANIZATIONS

Little League International Headquarters
P.O. Box 3485
Williamsport, PA 17701
(570) 326-1921
Web site: *www.littleleague.org*
This is the worldwide organization of teams for young baseball players.

PONY Baseball and Softball International Headquarters
300 Clare Drive
Washington, PA 15301
(724) 225-1060
Web site: *www.pony.org/ysnim/home/index.jsp*

RESOURCES

WEB SITES

Hitting for Excellence
www.hitting.com/advice1.htm
This Web site has plenty of hitting advice.

National College Athletic Association
www.ncaa.org/
Find school team schedules and view stats of your favorite teams and players.

INDEX

INDEX

About The Author

Ron Fitzgerald is a freelance writer living in New York City.